NOVELS BY M

For a complete list of Michelle's books:

www.MichelleFiles.com

ESCAPE THE DARK

A MYSTERY THRILLER

DARKNESS MYSTERY SERIES
BOOK ONE

MICHELLE FILES

Edited by
CECILY BROOKES

INTRODUCTION

Don't hitchhike, because the person who picks you up could be a serial killer.

Don't pick up hitchhikers, because they might be your worst nightmare.

What if three of them came together to form one terrifying night?

Get your copy of this gripping thriller novella.

Warning: Don't read it alone in the dark.

Copyright © 2022 by Michelle Files

All rights reserved. No part of this publication may be reproduced, distributed, or transmitted in any form, without prior written permission of the author.

Published by
The Author Files

This is a work of fiction. Any similarities to actual people, places or events is purely coincidental.

1st Edition 2022

CHAPTER 1

HARRIETT

"Just what I need," I said out loud as the rain began drizzling on the windshield of my car. I flicked the wiper lever up one notch. It was just enough to clear the windshield for a minute or so before I would need to do it again.

It was late. Really much too late to be out driving, especially in the rain. But I had just completed a long week of work and wanted to be home, in my own bed. I hated hotels, and never slept very well. People walking through the halls late at night, having loud conversations with no regard for those trying to sleep, were the worst. Yeah, I really hated hotels.

So on this dark, drizzly night, I decided to brave the elements, and my sleepiness, and drive all the way home. It was about an eight hour drive from the conference, to my home in San Diego. And with potty breaks and some food stops occasionally, that would probably turn it into a ten hour drive. I knew it was not going to be an easy night. I would be arriving in the wee hours of the morning, but I didn't care. My bed beckoned.

Besides, the long drive home would be all mine. I could be alone with my thoughts and sing along with the radio to my heart's content.

The low lying clouds abruptly split open, letting loose an immense amount of rain. Flashes of white lightning and tumultuous thunder followed. I had to slow down. It was difficult to see through the rain and the dark night. I leaned forward in my seat, as if that was going to give me a better view. It didn't.

"Why are there no street lights anywhere?" I muttered out loud.

The noise from the pounding of the rain on the windshield, the drumming on the roof of the car, along with the constant droning of the road, caused me to turn up the radio.

I stifled a yawn and rubbed my eyes, which were sore and tired from the monotony of staring at the road for so long. It seemed to never end. Perhaps trying to drive all the way home in one night wasn't such a great idea after all.

Without taking my eyes off the road, I reached my right hand into my purse that was resting in the passenger seat. Digging around before landing on what I was looking for, I retrieved my glasses and put them on. They helped a little, but not really much. It seemed as if the horrible visibility was not going to get much better.

Needing a break from the monotony of driving in the rain and having to keep a deep concentration on the road before me, I pulled off the highway, into the nearest convenience store. I pulled right up to the gas pump closest to the front of the store. Because I traveled a lot for work, I made it a habit to always get gas whenever I made a pitstop, even if all I needed was a tiny bit. No point in making extra stops for gas when I didn't have to. Besides, being a woman traveling alone, I didn't want to take any chances of running out of gas in the middle of nowhere. Especially not on a night like this one.

I pulled my hair back into a pony tail with a rubber hair tie and piled it on top of my head in a sort of messy bun thing. My long brown hair was going to get soaked out there, so I figured I would get it up and out of the way before it was stuck to my head. I'm a bit of a big woman, yeah I can admit that, though I'm not huge by any means. If I could just lose fifty pounds or so, I would be just right. That's not so easy to do. I've tried all the diets out there, none seem to work. Well, maybe they would work if I could stick to them, but willpower is not something I've ever had much of. And at 40 years old, I figure why bother? Lumbering out of the car, I swiped my credit card in the gas pump.

Once the gas was pumping into my car, I jogged for the store, trying to get out of the rain as quickly as possible. A potty break and some caffeine was exactly what the doctor ordered.

I couldn't help but notice the girl sitting on the curb just outside the store entrance. She was shielded from the rain by the overhang of the store, but the poor girl was still very soggy. It was obvious that she had been out in the rain for quite some time. I gave the girl a quick nod and walked on by. She couldn't have been more than 15 or 16, and was shivering.

But even more so than her age, was her demeanor and even her face. That poor face of hers. She was hunched over, her face was bruised and battered. She didn't even try to hide the blood on the front of her shirt. A wave of dizziness swept over me. I never did like the sight of blood.

I walked on by. The girl was none of my business. She seemed to be waiting for someone anyway. Surely they would be by soon. A parent, a sibling, a friend. I was sure she wouldn't be out in the cold for long.

After using the facilities and walking over to the coffee section of the store, I hesitated. The poor girl outside was on my mind. I couldn't leave her out there like that. Turning, I walked back out the front door, sans coffee.

"Um, hi," I said to the girl. "Would you like some hot chocolate? You look really cold and wet out here."

The girl nodded rapidly. "Yes, that would be great. Thanks."

I smiled and returned to the coffee counter, pouring myself a cup and getting a large hot chocolate for the teen.

Upon returning outside, the girl stood and took the cup from me. Her smile was sort of sad and grateful at the same time. "Thanks."

"Of course. What are you doing out here all alone this late? And in the rain? If you don't mind me asking." I looked closely at her face and the short crop of blonde hair that seemed to be sticking up everywhere. I was pretty sure she hadn't taken a shower in a while. In a good while, was my guess. My eyes traveled down to the blood stain on her shirt. Looking back up into her eyes, I asked, "Are you all right? Is someone coming to get you?"

The girl took a sip of the delicious warm liquid. "Um…my boyfriend…he…I'm trying to get back home. I ran out of money and can't take the bus. It's a long story."

That seemed to be all the girl wanted to reveal about herself. I understood. I was a random stranger, why would the girl tell me anything else?

"I see. Where are you going?" I asked, knowing that my question might be met with resistance.

"San Diego. Black River specifically. That's where I'm from."

I smiled. "That's where I'm heading. Well, San Diego

anyway. Black River is right on the way. I know you don't know me, and maybe this is a really bad idea, but I can't leave you sitting out here all night. Would you like a ride? I can't possibly leave you out here all alone."

I watched as the girl sized me up. She must have thought that I looked nice enough. It was obvious that she knew getting into a car with a complete stranger was a bad idea. A really bad idea. But, anything was better than being out in the freezing rain, and possibly hiding from an abusive boyfriend. "Yeah, sure. That would be great. I don't have any money for gas though."

I waved my hand in her direction. "That's totally unnecessary. Come on, let's go. This weather doesn't seem to be letting up at all."

The girl followed me to the car. I opened the trunk and unzipped my suitcase, pulling out a t-shirt. "This will be big on you, but here," I said, handing the shirt to the girl. She took it with a nod.

"Throw your pack in the back and sit up front with me, if you like. I'll turn the heater on full blast. Hopefully it won't take long for you to dry out."

Once I pulled back out onto the highway, I spoke first, hoping to lighten things up a bit. "I'm Harriett, by the way."

"Hi, I'm Autumn." She pulled off her bloody shirt, tossing it into the floorboard of the backseat. She slipped on the clean t-shirt and smiled. "Thank you for this. I really do appreciate it."

I stifled a laugh at the huge t-shirt on the skinny girl. The way it hung loosely, it could have been a dress on her.

"Not a problem at all, Autumn. That's a pretty name. So, we have a lot of hours ahead of us. You want to tell me why a young girl like you is out hitchhiking all alone?"

"I wasn't hitchhiking. I was just sitting," Autumn told me. "I don't hitchhike."

I smiled to myself. "You know that you are hitchhiking as we speak, right?"

"No, I'm not. I was just sitting there, minding my own business. You offered me a ride and I took it. My thumb was nowhere to be seen."

"Yeah, if you say so."

CHAPTER 2

HARRIETT

It seemed as if the two of us were starting out our journey together in a bit of a disagreement. Neither of us spoke for a good twenty minutes.

Finally, I broke the silence. "You know, I've never picked up a hitchhiker before."

Autumn gave me the side eye, without speaking.

"I know, I know, sorry. You weren't hitchhiking. I should have said that I've never given a stranger a ride before. So…" I continued, "how were you planning on getting home? And where were you planning to sleep tonight?"

"You ask a lot of questions."

I had to concede that one. "I suppose I do. But teenage girls shouldn't be out all alone. It worries me. There are a lot of bad people out there. I could be a serial killer for all you know."

Autumn tilted her head. "So, are you a serial killer?"

"Do you think I would tell you if I were?" I replied. "Besides, maybe you are the serial killer."

Autumn turned back to watch the rain out the front windshield. "Yeah maybe."

I couldn't help but laugh. In spite of our strange circumstances, I liked Autumn. There was just something about the girl.

"We'll stop in a little while and get something to eat. My treat," I told her. Reaching over to the heater dial, I turned it up a bit more. "You are shivering."

I left the girl alone while she sipped her hot chocolate, staring out the front window. It looked as if she had a lot on her mind, not even acknowledging my presence after that.

A few minutes later, I glanced over to see that Autumn had fallen asleep. Her head rested against the passenger window. Her mouth hung open.

Poor thing. She's probably exhausted. Oh, the innocence of the young. Little did she know what she had gotten herself in for. I mean, who in their right mind would get into a car with a total stranger in the middle of the night and then just fall asleep?

Bad idea. Really bad idea.

I could hardly contain my excitement. The problem was that there was no fun in killing a sleeping person. She wouldn't fight. She would show no terror. She wouldn't even beg for her life. Where was the joy in that? Nowhere, that's where.

She would wake up eventually. That's when things would get interesting. My entire body shivered at the thought.

I continued driving into the darkness. The rain and gloom seemed completely suitable for this night.

An hour or so later, Autumn woke abruptly. She sat straight up in her seat, looking around inside the car. When her eyes landed on me, she let out a calming breath and her shoulders relaxed.

"Hey there. Did you sleep well?" I asked, knowing that she had. Her snoring made sure that I knew her status at all times.

"Um, yeah, I guess." She squinted as she leaned forward, trying to get a better look out the front windshield. "Where are we?"

"Well, if I remember correctly, we should be just around the bend from this cheesy diner I've driven by several times. I've never stopped there though, so this will be a new adventure for the both of us."

"Okay, good, I need to use the bathroom."

"Yep, there it is."

We both stared at the obnoxious flashing neon sign depicting a fat pink pig wearing a chef's hat and devouring a large turkey leg. It made both of us laugh.

The inside of the restaurant was a bit more subdued, but not much. The walls were lime green and peach colored. It almost hurt my eyes to look at it. Pigs were obviously the theme, as there were dozens, if not hundreds, of photos and cartoons adorning the walls.

Good god, what have I gotten myself into here?

I found us a table while Autumn went to find the ladies room. A portly woman in her mid-sixties brought me two menus and two glasses of water. She had shortly cropped, gray hair, and a stubby nose. I stifled a snicker at the comparison between her and their decorating choices. I wondered if she owned the joint.

I looked over our choices, while waiting. Ten minutes later, Autumn finally emerged. She looked like she had washed her face. Her hair was damp.

"Did you take a bath in there?" I asked with a smirk. I mean, who does that in a diner bathroom?

She side eyed me as she took her seat. "No, I didn't take a bath." Her tone was not lost on me. "I just cleaned up a little. I've been on the road for several days and haven't had a shower. Is that all right with you?" That time she didn't even try to disguise her annoyance with me.

"Of course. Sorry."

She picked up her menu and perused it.

Once our waitress had taken our orders, we had nothing to do but be forced to talk to each other.

"So...what's it like living in Black River?" I asked her.

She gave me a half shrug. "It's fine, I guess."

"What about the River Killer?" I continued.

"Well it's not me, if that's what you're asking."

I threw my head back and laughed. "You are much too young. It obviously couldn't be you."

The River Killer was a notorious serial killer who had been terrorizing the small town of Black River for over three decades. He had never been caught, and was still killing, even to this day.

Now, I know what you are thinking. And no, it isn't me either. I guess that I'm technically old enough, if I had started killing as a child, but I didn't. I was 16 when I killed my first person, and that one was kind of an accident. Well, mostly anyway.

CJ had asked me out for a Friday night. He was cute, and I said yes. The problem was that he wanted a lot more than I was willing to give him that night. He parked up by the cliffs. When I jumped out of his car to get away from him, he took chase. He caught me and a struggle ensued. At one point, I slugged him, causing him to lose his balance. He fell, his head landing hard on a tree that had fallen years earlier. His neck broke instantly.

I never told anyone that I was involved. I had told my parents that I was going out with friends. They didn't want me to date. The police figured that he was up there alone, or at least they could find nothing to disprove that, and it was all just chalked up to an unfortunate accident.

That first kill, accident that it was, opened something up inside of me. Though I was somewhat shocked and disgusted at what happened to CJ, it kind of made me tingle inside. After that, I killed others. Just occasionally, nothing like the prolific works of the River Killer, but I held my own. At last count, there were twelve. Not a bad number. One I was kind of proud of.

And now, here I was, with a cute young thing who would no doubt never see the town of Black River again. I had other plans for her.

CHAPTER 3

HARRIETT

"They haven't caught the River Killer, have they?" I asked Autumn.

She narrowed her eyes at me. "No, Harriett, they haven't caught him. Don't you think that would be national news? Hell, international news, I suspect. This has been going on for over thirty years now. I can't go a day, no matter where I am, without hearing something about that jackass. Whenever someone hears that I'm from Black River, it's all they want to talk about. I'm just over it all at this point."

I nodded. "Yeah, I get that. I'm sure it gets old. Just morbid curiosity, I guess. Sorry."

"No, I'm sorry. I'm just tired and cranky, I suppose. I do understand why people ask. If I didn't live there, and didn't hear about that guy every single day, I would probably be curious too. You are being really nice in giving me a ride, and buying me dinner, that I shouldn't take out my crankiness on you." Autumn gave me a contrite smile.

I realized that I needed to not piss off the girl. I needed her to want to continue traveling with me. This was imperative. If she decided that I was annoying, or just not worth her time, she might bail on me. I couldn't let that happen.

No matter what.

"You know what? It's all good. Don't worry about it. We can totally talk about something else, if you like," I told her. "Tell me about yourself."

I suffered through her long diatribe about her childhood, and about how her mother didn't understand her. She took off to see friends two weeks ago and never told her mother where she was going. She knew that her mother would be angry when she arrived back home, but that was her mother's problem, as far as Autumn was concerned.

I learned way more about the girl than I really ever wanted to. None of it was important, none of it mattered at all. She would never make it home anyway. Her mother would not be angry, she would just never know what happened to her. I would make sure of that. But then again, I always felt all kinds of happy inside when one of my 'friends' was found and they couldn't figure out who did it. That was the ultimate joy. Nothing on earth compared to that feeling of euphoria.

After our meals of pulled pork sandwiches, (what else would we have eaten at that particular establishment?), we headed back out on the road. The rain had let up a bit by then, but it was still coming down. In the dark, I had to slow down and squint into the night to navigate those back roads that I was so fond of.

CHAPTER 4

AUTUMN

I can't believe how utterly stupid that Harriett woman is. She even had the nerve to ask me if I had taken a bath in the restaurant. Seriously, what did she expect? I looked a mess and needed to freshen up a bit. Being on the road was grimy business. God, I could just kill her right now.

Yeah, I said it. I could kill her.

And if I didn't need a ride home so badly, I might have done just that. But no, that's a really bad idea. Even I knew that.

But, I could kill her and take her car. Hmmm…perhaps. No, just no. It was easier to get away with murder than grand theft auto.

I should know. About the murder part anyway. I had killed several people. Yeah, yeah, I know, I'm only 16. So what? Sixteen year olds can kill. So can 11 year olds, which is exactly how old I was the first time.

It was my mother's 'boyfriend.' Why do I put emphasis on

the word 'boyfriend?' That would be because she hadn't known him very long, and let the lech move in with us. She did that a lot. I lost count over the years of how many there were. Five or six. Maybe even a dozen. Who knows at this point.

One thing I do know is that he was a perv and a lech. He thought that it was perfectly okay to fondle little girls. But you know what? He only did that once. The second time he came after me, I was prepared. Earlier that day, I had snuck into the kitchen when they were watching TV and drinking beer. A lot of beer. I took out a small knife. Remember, I was only 11 and something like four foot eight or so. A large butcher knife would have been overkill for me. Pun intended. A small knife would do.

My mother worked at a local hospital in San Diego. She wasn't a nurse or anything. She worked as a night janitor. She worked the graveyard shift while I slept. Usually that was in the room next to whichever perv she had living with us at the time. The thing about my mother was that she didn't like being alone. She needed a man to validate her. During the scant few times that she was between men, she moped around the house and drank. A lot. Still…it was better than the alternative.

Now don't get me wrong. A few times she did manage to bring home a decent guy. One who would treat her right and was nice to me. But they never lasted long. A few weeks in, she would show her true colors, which weren't pretty, and they'd be gone in a flash. My mother was probably bipolar. No one had ever diagnosed her, but I could see it. For a few days, she would be all flighty and happy and out shopping like money was no object. Then almost as suddenly, she seemed to go into a deep depression. She would mope around the house, if she got out of bed at all, and I would have to fend for myself. Even as a small child, I had to learn to make my own food, or I would starve. I made sandwiches for my mother and practically had to force her to eat them. Yeah, my five year old self was keeping both of us alive.

No wonder I was so screwed up.

Back to the lech. My mother left for work one night, and left me alone with him. That's where it all went wrong. I swear that it was not more than ten minutes after she walked out the door and he was standing in my bedroom. He dropped his pants as I did my best to pretend to sleep.

Need I go into the gory details of what happened next? No, really it's not necessary. Just suffice it to say that he came for me, and I used that small knife. The man died right there on my bedroom floor. I told the police what happened, with every word being the truth. The fact that his pants were lying on the floor next to his body was a big help in the matter.

As it turned out, he was a registered sex offender, and should never have been allowed anywhere near me. Did my mother look into that? No, of course she didn't. In fact, she blamed me for what happened. Yeah, an 11 year old child was to blame for a pedophile coming at me. Mother of the Year, she definitely was not.

So, of course, the next question is why in the world do I want to go back to live with that woman?

I don't. I would never live with her again. In fact, my prayers were answered only days ago when I found out that she had died. Yeah I know, that's harsh. But you didn't know the woman. I did. The world is a better place without her in it.

Where is my father, you ask? Well, that's the good news. Once my mother died, her sister told me who my father is. She even contacted him and told him about me. He had no idea that I existed. So typical of my mother.

He called me and we made plans. He still lived in the San Diego area and wants me to come live with him. So…that's where I'm going. I figure that my aunt was so helpful in getting us together because she didn't want me ending up on her doorstep. Fantastic family I have, huh?

Sitting there in the car, I was concentrating on the beads of rain hopping across the windshield. It had let up a bit, and I was keeping an eye on the darkness ahead. Harriett was yammering on as I focused on other things. She didn't seem to notice that I was not participating in the conversation at all.

The high beams caught the reflective surface of the yellow sign indicating an upcoming sharp turn ahead of us. Harriett was driving a bit too fast for my taste and I instinctively grabbed onto the passenger door grip next to me. Thankfully, Harriett eased her foot off of the accelerator as we entered the curve. Being in the middle of nowhere, the last thing we needed was to slip off the wet road and into the embankment. It was much too dark, wet, and cold out there to have to deal with that nonsense.

I assumed that Harriett had a phone with her, but had no idea if service was even available in the area. My mother wouldn't pay for a phone for me, and I certainly couldn't afford one, so I traveled without one. I always laughed at the shocked looks on people's faces when they found out that I didn't carry a phone with me every waking moment, like they did. I guess that I'm old fashioned in that way. I know I'm still a teenager, but I really never found the need to have one. I never had many friends, so who was I going to call anyway?

If we did have an accident, waiting for another car to come by and help us, was probably not going to happen. Since I had been riding along, there had only been one car on that lonely road. But I had a gut feeling that no matter how many cars had been out there, no one would be willing to stop and help someone on the side of the road in the middle of the night, in that weather.

So, if we ended up in a ditch, we would have to spend a freezing night in the car. I've slept in worse places.

Coming around a bend, some movement caught my eye. It looked like a dark figure shuffling along the narrow shoulder. His back was to us, and it was difficult to make him out in the dark. He seemed oblivious to the fact that we were coming up alongside him. Perhaps many cars had done so, without even slowing down to see if he needed any help. Yeah, that was almost definitely the case.

As we passed, I turned in my seat to watch him. He noticed us then. With one arm wrapped in front of him, to stave off the chill of the rain, he stuck his right thumb out. With a quick glance, he looked to be not much older than I was. His loose fitting clothing was drenched and his hair was plastered to his head.

Harriett continued driving and tapped the accelerator as we pulled out of the curve. She knew better than to pull over and give a male stranger a ride. Especially in the middle of the night, rain or not.

I wondered if his car had broken down and he was just trying to get to the nearest place to call someone. Or maybe he had been in an accident. There was no way to know without speaking with him.

"Stop!" I yelled out.

CHAPTER 5

AUTUMN

Harriett hit the brakes and pulled to the side of the road. It was an abrupt maneuver and if my arm hadn't shot out and gripped the dashboard in front of me, my forehead surely would have. Wet gravel crunched beneath the tires as she rolled to a stop, and put the car in 'Park.'

"What? Why do you want me to stop?" she asked me, her lips were set in a tight straight line. "This better be good."

I pointed toward the rear of the car. "So we can pick up that guy we just passed."

She hit the radio button, silencing the car and turned in her seat to peer out the back window. "What guy?"

"The one hitchhiking. You didn't see him?" I asked her. Obviously she hadn't.

"You must have fallen asleep and been dreaming. There was no one there, and I don't see anyone now. Believe me, I'm watching the road carefully." She turned back around and reached down to the center console to grab the gear shift. "Let's go. I want to get home at a decent hour tonight."

"I wasn't dreaming. I was wide awake and staring out the front of the car. He was definitely there. We can't leave him out in this weather. It wouldn't be right." I placed my hand over hers, stopping her from putting it into 'Drive.' "Please, there is someone out there."

Before she had a chance to start the forward progress of the car once again, I opened my door and stepped out into the rain. It was as if the skies had decided to open up, right then and there. I was drenched within a couple of seconds. Not having the forethought to put on a jacket, I wrapped my arms in front of myself to keep warm. It wasn't working, but I would only be out in the weather for a minute. I would survive. I began walking toward the rear of the car. Suddenly, I was unsure if what I had told Harriett was accurate. Had I dozed off with the monotony of the car motion and road in front of us, and actually been dreaming? Squinting, I didn't see anyone in the dark night.

Okay, she was right. I was imagining things. I turned to get back into the warm car that was beckoning me.

"Hey! Wait!"

I turned at the voice. He seemed to emerge from absolutely nowhere. One second the night was just a void. The next second, he was only a few feet from where I stood.

Before I had a chance to say anything, he continued. "Did you pull over for me?"

His sad, puppy dog eyes won me over in an instant. The poor man, boy actually, was drenched from head to toe. So was I, really. But he was shivering and pale. I wasn't sure he would survive the night out in the storm.

"Yes, get in the backseat and out of this weather," I ordered.

I didn't have to tell him twice. He practically flew into the backseat. Harriett's eyes widened as the stranger seemed to bring the dampness of the night in with him. I watched as she shuddered.

"Close the door. Hurry, you are letting in the rain," Harriett ordered.

"Sorry about your car. It's getting soaked," he told us. "Do you have a towel maybe?"

"No towel," Harriett replied. "But don't worry about it. I'll turn up the heat. You and the car will be toasty in no time."

He smiled and leaned back in his seat. The overhead light illuminated his features.

He was young, probably not much older than I was. I guessed him to be somewhere between 17 and 20. He wore jeans and a t-shirt, which had seen better days. The shirt was faded and threadbare. It had a hole in the seam where the sleeve met the actual shirt. A dirty yellow bandana was tied around his neck and hung loosely.

Though a bit ragged from his travels, he was cute, with light brown skin. He was also thin. Very thin. Hitchhiking will do that to a person. Generally, money was not plentiful for large meals. I too, had lost weight. His dark brown eyes seemed a bit haunted. I don't really know what that means, but the word seemed appropriate.

However, the first thing I noticed when he got into the car was not his looks, it was the scent that wafted in with him. It was musky. But not just that. It was a dirty, sweaty sort of scent. Gamey might be a better description. After being on the road awhile, I was familiar with that scent. It came through loud and clear, even in the drenching rain. It told me that he had also been on the road awhile, and that there had been no hot showers for him in the recent past.

I ignored the smell. It would be rude not to. Glancing over at Harriett, I could see that she had also noticed it. She wrinkled up her nose, but said nothing as she gave me wide eyes. That was her not so subtle way of telling me that she didn't appreciate what came in from out in the night.

"Why are you out in this weather?" I asked. "Did your car break down?" I was pretty sure that wasn't the case. It was the same reason I was out. No car. Not enough bus money. Wanting to get home.

He shrugged. "No one was giving me a ride. I had no choice but to walk. You know how it is." He looked at me knowingly.

I did. Though, being a female was pretty helpful in obtaining rides. People didn't seem as suspicious of us as they were of some lone male walking the roads and looking haggard.

"Do you two know each other?" Harriett asked, as she switched on her left blinker, glanced into the side mirror, and quietly pulled back onto the road.

"Why do you ask that?" I responded, glancing back at our new friend.

She shrugged, reaching over and turning the heater up to full blast for the young man. "I don't know. You are both hitchhiking and are going in the same direction. Just wondering."

"Yeah, because all of us travelers know each other, sheesh." God, what an idiot she was.

Harriett turned and glared at me. If looks could kill… Ha, probably a poor choice of words. I laughed. Harriett didn't even ask me why.

I turned back to face our guest in the back seat. "I'm Autumn, and this here is Harriett." I gestured toward the driver's seat.

"I'm Jose."

"Nice to meet you," I responded. "So, where are you headed, Jose?" I asked him.

"San Diego."

I smiled. "Hey, us too. Tonight is your lucky night."

Harriett glared over at me. I was getting the feeling that she wasn't too happy with our new passenger. I really don't know why though. What's one more? We were all going the same way. I just couldn't leave him out there in the wet, freezing night. He wouldn't survive it. Of that, I was pretty sure.

Of course, with me around, he might not survive in this car either. I smiled. But no, he was fine. Harriett on the other hand...

"So, Jose," I began, "you ever been to Black River?"

"Yeah, hasn't everyone?"

"You'd be surprised how many people avoid the town like it's got the black plague," I replied.

"I can't really blame them. Have you been there?" he asked me.

"I live there."

His eyebrows shot up. "Really? Aren't you afraid of the River Killer?"

There it was. I just couldn't get away from the topic of the River Killer. I shrugged. "I guess. But I don't let him rule my life. I do what I want." I smiled back at Jose.

He didn't respond.

"You warm enough back there?" Harriett asked him.

"Yeah, I'm good. I'm starting to thaw out. Man, it's rough out there. Hitchhiking is not for the faint of heart," he told us.

"Why are you hitchhiking anyway?" I asked.

"Probably the same reason you were hitchhiking," Harriett interjected.

I glared over at her. That woman was seriously getting on my nerves. I answered her through gritted teeth. "I told you before that I wasn't hitchhiking. I was just sitting on the curb

MICHELLE FILES

when you offered me a ride, and I took it. That isn't hitchhiking."

"Yeah, whatever you say," Harriett said. The annoyance in her voice shown through.

"Sounds like hitchhiking to me," Jose muttered from the back seat.

Harriett laughed. "Told ya."

I scowled at the both of them. "Whatever." I crossed my arms in front of myself and turned to stare out the front window. Engaging with the two of them no longer interested me.

About an hour later, I turned around to our friend in the back seat. "You never answered my question."

His eyes sort of meandered open.

"Oh, sorry. I didn't realize you were asleep."

"It's fine. What question?" he asked.

"Why are you hitchhiking?"

"Oh, no big reason, really. I'm just seeing the country."

"Do you live in San Diego?" I persisted.

"No. I used to, but my mom and I moved to Texas a couple years ago. I'm going back to see some friends."

"Oh. Is your mom still in Texas?" I asked.

He shrugged. "Who knows. I haven't talked to her in a while. We aren't that close."

"Oh. I'm sorry to hear that," I replied.

I watched his face, expecting some sort of explanation, but he didn't seem to want to elaborate. I turned back to face the windshield. None of my business, I figured.

"Can we stop at a convenience store soon?" I asked. "I need to pee and get something to drink."

CHAPTER 6

JOSE

Thank god. Stopping somewhere...anywhere...would be preferable to the insufferable boredom of these two people. Unfortunately, I was forced to endure them to get where I was going.

I jumped out the moment the car pulled up to the gas pumps. No need to wait around. I had no intention of offering gas money. Thankfully, no one asked.

After finishing up in the bathroom, I wandered around the store, looking for something to eat. Landing on some burritos that were being kept under a heating lamp, they seemed good enough. No telling how long they had been under that lamp, since they looked a bit underwhelming, but I figured they would do. I didn't have a lot of money, and you know what they say about beggars not being choosers.

I grabbed two of the questionable burritos and headed to the glass refrigerated cases. Just as I grabbed a cheap bottle of water, I saw Autumn out of the corner of my eye filling two large soda cups. Her head turned left, then right, looking around to see if anyone was watching her. I was, but she didn't see me behind the cases of beer stacked at least five feet tall. I was crouched behind them. She seemed to be acting suspiciously for someone who was just getting a couple of drinks from the fountain.

I watched as she reached into her purse and pulled out a small metal container. Once again, she glanced around. The store was mostly deserted and no one paid her any mind. She opened the container and poured something into one of the drinks.

That was interesting. Now the question was, whose drink was it? Was it her own, and she wanted to add a little pep, or even some medication to her drink? That wasn't completely unreasonable. I, myself, had been known to add a little somethin' somethin' to my own drinks now and again.

Or was it Harriett's drink that Autumn was doctoring? And was Harriett aware of that fact? I'm guessing not. So... what in the world was Autumn up to? She was up to no good, if you ask me.

I continued watching her. Autumn used a straw to stir the doctored drink, then quickly placed lids on both of them. She then walked over to the candy aisle and perused it. I noticed that she was careful to keep track of which drink was in which hand.

I decided it was time to step in. She was bent over looking carefully at the chocolate section. "Hey there."

Autumn jumped and almost lost control of her soda cups. She turned to face me. "Geez, you scared me."

"Here," I reached for the cups, "let me help you with those."

She pulled them in closer to her body. "No, it's okay. I got 'em."

"I'm happy to help." I took hold of them and removed

them from her grasp. She released them reluctantly. "Now you have free hands to get yourself some candy."

I looked down at the cups. "Which one is yours and which one Harriett's? Or are they the same? I'll keep them sorted." My mind reeled. This should be fun.

"Um," she pointed. "That one there is mine. Thanks."

She turned back around and quickly grabbed a candy bar, barely looking away from me. It seemed as if she kept one eye on me and the cups I had control of, at all times. "This will do." She reached for the cups again. "I'll take those. I need to go pay."

I pulled them away from her grasp. "I'll carry them to the counter for you. No problem."

I could see in her eyes that I was driving her crazy. She wanted to hang onto the sodas, and obviously keep track of which was which. I knew which was which. I knew what I was doing. I smiled as I turned away from her.

She probably thought I had a crush on her. I didn't. "Yeah, okay," she reluctantly agreed, leading the way to the checkout counter. She had no idea if the cups were still in the same hands or not, by the time we got to the cashier.

I knew.

After paying, she took the sodas from my hands, and I let her. "Thank you for your help," she told me.

"No problem. You just had a lot of things to carry."

We ducked our heads, as if it would help keep us dry, and jogged back to the car where Harriett was waiting. It wasn't raining too much at the moment, but it was still very cold out. The two together were not a fun combination.

From the back seat, I watched Autumn hand Harriett her soda. Autumn seemed satisfied with that action. I still didn't know if the substance was put in Harriett's drink or not. I figured I would find out soon enough.

"So…Autumn," I began, "tell me what it's like living in Black River."

She took a drink from her straw. The action seemed a bit tentative, as if she wasn't entirely sure if she should be drinking out of that cup or not. I bit my upper lip.

"What do you want to know?" she asked.

"You know what I want to know. The Black River Killer, of course. What's going on with that?"

She shrugged. "How should I know. I'm not a cop."

I laughed. "Yeah, I figured that. I was just wondering what the gossip was like. Do people in town think they know who the killer might be? Is anyone harassed by anyone who lives there? And has anyone been questioned, or even arrested as a suspect?"

Autumn turned to look at me. "Seriously? That's a lot of questions. And I don't know the answer to any of them."

My shoulders slumped. I really was disappointed. I was hoping for some juicy gossip. "Maybe you are the River Killer," I added with a chuckle.

"Yeah, maybe. I'm sixteen, but have been killing people for over thirty years. Yep, that sounds about right."

A snort escaped before I could stop it.

"The truth is," she continued, "that I pay very little attention to what goes on in that stupid town. I hate Black River and want to move out as soon as I can."

"Why is that?" I asked.

"I don't know. I grew up there and it's boring. And every single year, my mother drags me to that stupid mass funeral service they have. It's the worst."

I sat up in my seat. "Oh yeah, I sort of remember hearing something about that. What's that all about?" I asked her.

"Well, a bunch of years ago, apparently everyone in town decided they would have an annual memorial service for all the Black River victims. Nobody asked me, of course. So, my mother dragged me there every year. I hated every single minute of it," Autumn told us. "Usually the sheriff gives a speech and some of the family members of the victims get up and say something. But you know what? It's mostly a social hour. After everyone does their bit up on the stage, the town just stands around talking and laughing and eating. There is always a potluck involved. I swear, it's just an excuse for the town to have a party. I think it's all in bad taste. But like I said, no one asked me for my opinion."

"Interesting," I replied. "I wonder if the River Killer attends the service?"

We both turned to Harriett when she seemed to choke on the chips she was eating. She raised her hand. "I'm fine. Sorry. Continue with your conversation."

Autumn shrugged. "Yeah, the killer probably does attend the service. Since pretty much everyone in town is there. It might draw attention to him if he never showed up. People might notice."

"That's true," I responded. I turned to our driver. "What about you, Harriett? Do you also live in Black River?"

"No way," she replied. "And I stay as far as I possibly can from that place. It gives me the creeps."

"Yeah, I get that."

"I guess I've been driving too long. I'm starting to feel a bit sleepy," Harriett told us.

My eyes instantly darted over to Autumn. She didn't react at all. Hmmm.

Autumn was concentrating on the road unfolding in front of her. All of a sudden, she gasped.

CHAPTER 7

AUTUMN

"Harriett! Watch out!" I screamed as a small animal, a squirrel maybe, scurried into the road, directly in our path. He stopped in the middle of the road as if frozen in place, staring at the car headed right for him. I could only imagine the rapid beating of the poor creature's heart at that moment.

Harriett slammed on the brakes and pulled the steering wheel hard to the right in an attempt at sparing the little guy's life. As we barreled toward the side of the road, and a bunch of large rocks, I saw the critter continue on his way and disappear over the edge.

Harriett failed to get the car to stop in time and we slammed into the rocks. I was slammed against the seatbelt I was wearing. Hard. It almost felt like it cut me in two. Apparently her old car didn't have air bags.

Harriett gasped next to me. "Are you all right?" I asked her.

"Um..." She was taking shallow breaths. "Yeah, I...think so. You?"

"I'm fine. I might have a broken rib though." I gasped as a sharp pain seemed to pierce right through me with just the slightest movement. If I didn't know any better, I would have thought someone was stabbing me. Yeah, it hurt that badly. Thank god for the seatbelt. It could have been worse. Way worse.

Jose began moaning in the back seat. I removed my seatbelt and turned to see if he was all right, flinching once again from the stabbing pain in my rib area. I found him crumpled in the floorboard. He was trying to get up, but not moving very quickly as he did.

"Jose!" I got up on the seat on my knees and reached over to help him. I took a hold of the back of his sweatshirt and pulled. I don't think it helped much. "Are you okay?"

"I think so," he mumbled, as he detangled himself from the heap he had ended up in on the floor. I watched as he eventually managed to get himself back up on the seat. He was rubbing his head.

"Are you hurt?" I asked. "Weren't you wearing a seatbelt?"

"No, I wasn't wearing a seatbelt," he snarled at me, while rubbing a spot on the side of his head.

"Well, I'm glad you are okay," I replied, rolling my eyes and letting out a huff of breath as I did so.

"What the hell happened?" Jose asked Harriett directly.

"Something ran...out in the road...in front of me." Her delivery was slow and a bit slurred, as if she were having a hard time getting the proper words out. The corner of my lips curled upward.

"I think you gave me a concussion," Jose added.

Harriett gave Jose a glare, which I'm pretty sure he didn't see. "Something ran out in front of me."

"Yeah, you already said that," he replied.

"Um," I said, looking directly at Jose, "shouldn't someone get out and see if the car is all right?"

His eyes widened. "Me? Why Me? Because I'm the guy? Why don't you get out? I'm just along for the ride."

"Yeah, me too," I told him. "It's not my car."

We both turned to Harriett. She didn't look so great. Her eyes were unfocused. It looked like she was about to pass out at any moment.

"Harriett, are you all right?" I asked.

"I'm, um…I don't know. I think I hit my head."

"Did she hit her head or did you give her something?" Jose asked me directly.

"I…what? What are you talking about?" I asked him.

"You know what I'm talking about." His tone was quite confrontational. "The soda cups from the store. I saw what you did."

Was he fishing? What did he actually think he saw? Should I press the issue? No, perhaps I shouldn't. I turned back around in my seat and watched the rain as it began to come down harder than it had been.

"Never mind," I spat out. "I'll go check on the car." I opened the car door and grimaced at the sharp pain as I began to climb out.

"Stop. I'll go."

I sat back down and closed the door, relief washing over me. Jose climbed out and disappeared into the dark wet night beyond. I was forever grateful that I didn't have to go out there in that weather. It was one of the few times that I liked the fact that a man took over and let me just sit in the warm dry car, while he took care of things. Normally I was the type to take charge and do things myself, never waiting on a man to do it. This time? I was fine with it.

I watched as the headlights lit up Jose, as he walked around to the front of the car, leaned over the huge rocks we had just run into, and looked at the front grill. He was already a soggy mess, rain water dribbled down his face.

Then he stepped over to the driver's side and knelt down, disappearing from view. A few seconds later he reappeared with a deep frown. That wasn't good. He walked past where Harriett was sitting and climbed back into the seat behind her. The wind caused me to shiver in the couple of seconds it took him to get the door closed.

"Well…the front grill is damaged. But that's not a big deal. The problem we have is that the driver's side tire is flat. I don't think the rim is bent, so hopefully a new tire is all we need. Harriett, do you have a spare?"

We both looked over at Harriett. She was fast asleep…or passed out…or hell, dead for all I knew.

"Harriett?" I asked, a bit tentatively.

Nothing.

"Harriett?" I was louder that time.

Still no response. I couldn't even tell if she was breathing or not. "Harriett!" I yelled, reaching over and gently shaking her on the shoulder.

That got her attention.

Her eyes flew open. "Whaaaa?" She blinked a few times, as if trying to get her wits about her.

"Are you all right?" I asked her.

"Yeah, I think so. I just can't seem to shake off this sleepiness. I feel like…I took a sleeping pill. My brain…is kinda… foggy."

Jose narrowed his eyes at me. "What?" I asked. "I did nothing with her soda. I don't know what you think you saw, but…"

"Yeah, right," he interrupted. "Whatever that was, I don't even care. She's not gonna be in any shape to drive, that's pretty obvious. So I guess one of us will have to do it. After the tire is changed, that is." He paused, as if for dramatic effect, looking at me for a reaction.

Did he seriously think I was going to go out into the dark, creepy night and change the tire on my own? And in the pouring rain? Um, nope. Not gonna happen. I would sit there in the car all night before even beginning to consider changing the tire.

"Well don't look at me. I have a broken rib." That was the truth at least. I rubbed my ribcage for dramatic effect.

"You do not," he challenged.

I let out an audible huff. "Believe what you want. But there's no way that I can lift up a tire, not to mention all the other stuff that goes with tire changing. I don't even know how. I've never changed a tire in my life."

That was true, I hadn't. But I knew how it was done. I wasn't a complete idiot. He didn't need to know that though.

He sat in that back seat for several minutes without responding. He knew that if he wanted the tire changed, he was going to have to do it. I refused to, and Harriett was out cold in the driver's seat.

CHAPTER 8

JOSE

"I don't freakin' believe this. I'm just a passenger, and apparently it's now my job to change the tire." I made no attempt to hide my annoyance at the situation.

Autumn turned back to face me. "Yeah, I'm just a passenger too. It's her car." Autumn indicated Harriett with just a quick tip of her head.

We both turned and watched Harriett for a moment. Her breathing was deep and steady. She definitely wasn't dead. Not yet anyway. But she was out cold. She wouldn't be of any help.

"Can you at least get out and help?" I asked Autumn, raising my eyebrows for emphasis.

"I told you, I have a broken rib. I can't lift anything."

Yeah, sure you do, I thought to myself. I rubbed the stubble on my face as I contemplated our current situation. It wasn't good. I was going to have to go out into the freezing rain, in the dark, and change the tire by myself. That was obvious. No was was willing, or conscious enough, to help me.

"Can you pop the trunk at least?" I snarked at Autumn.

"Yeah." Her eyes narrowed my way, but she complied. Autumn leaned over Harriett's lap and felt around the lower part of the instrument panel, near the driver's door. Harriett didn't stir even slightly. "I don't know where…oh, here it is!"

We both turned toward the trunk when it popped open. I steeled myself against the weather, and jumped out of the car. I was drenched before I reached the rear of the vehicle.

"They are so gonna pay for this," I mumbled to myself. It didn't matter what I said. There was no way anyone was going to hear me, because they wouldn't dare get out of their nice, warm cocoon.

I dug around in the trunk for the spare tire, lug wrench, and jack. I had to push aside a suitcase and backpack to find what I was looking for. Just as I got everything out and over to where I would need it, the rain let up. It turned into a drizzle. That was something I could deal with. Anything was better than the slog of water that had been coming at me before. I looked up toward the skies and silently thanked whoever it was that was responsible for easing up on the weather and giving me just a little bit of a reprieve. However, it was far from dry. The constant drizzle began grating on my nerves.

Before I began, I took another look up into the skies. The clouds were beginning to thin and I could see the full moon for the first time that night. Though the headlights were on, the lit up sky helped tremendously.

Out of the corner of my eye, I saw movement inside the car. Harriett was waking up and moving around just a bit. Autumn was talking to her, but I couldn't hear anything either one of them said. I didn't know exactly what it was, I couldn't quite pinpoint it, but I got a weird vibe from both of them.

And I still didn't know what was up with whatever it was that Autumn put in Harriett's drink. It clearly knocked her out, but for what purpose? It didn't kill the woman, so why do it? Why would anyone want the person driving the car they were riding in, to pass out? I mean, that could have been disastrous. What if she had passed out in the middle of a busy highway? As it was, she drove off the road and hit the damn rocks, causing me to be out dealing with the aftermath.

It was no longer pouring, but I was still soaked and freezing. A shiver ran up my spine as I continued watching the women, wondering if they were talking about me. When Autumn turned to watch me, I went back to my task.

CHAPTER 9

AUTUMN

"I wish he'd hurry up out there, I'm freezing." I reached over and turned up the heater dial to the highest setting, basking in the hot air pulling the chill from my body.

"Wha...wha did you...say?"

I looked over at Harriett with wide eyes, who seemed to be coming around. Damn, I didn't give her enough. I was hoping we were through with her. There was no reason why I couldn't drive the car the rest of the way.

Poison was usually my weapon of choice whenever I killed anyone. Sometimes killing was in the heat of the moment, and I used whatever I could, but poison was my favorite. I just loved how a body would writhe and convulse when poisoned. It made me all warm and gooey inside.

One time this old man, 50 at least, pulled over to give me a ride one late afternoon. Not ten minutes in, he pulled off the road and started to get handsy. I knew at that moment that the situation was not going to end well for one of us. As he was groping me, I managed to get my trusted army knife out of my purse. I never go anywhere without it. The man screamed like a little girl when the knife pierced through the side of his neck. And he bled. Man, he bled a lot. He managed to sit back up, while holding the side of his neck. The look in his eyes was a mixture of bewilderment and hatred. He had probably done that to lots of girls over the years. But I was the last one. I climbed out of that car quickly, somehow managing to get very little of the man's blood on my clothing. I stood and watched him slump over in the front seat and die.

I couldn't take his car. It was covered in the red stuff. So, I turned and headed back for the highway. That old man had actually made my day. Though poisoning would have been a lot more fun.

∽

As far as Harriett was concerned, I didn't have any poison on me at the moment. So, I had to improvise and give her something that would knock her out. With Jose in the car, I couldn't really just reach over and stab the woman, could I? I was just hoping that she would pass out and we could leave her body on the side of the road, to freeze solid overnight. A snicker escaped my lips and I quickly covered my mouth.

Then I'd have to get rid of Jose too. I was still working out how that would go.

"Hmm...what?" Harriett mumbled.

"Harriett? Are you all right?"

Her drowsy eyes turned to me. "What happ...happened?" She was having a tough time getting the words out.

"We had a car accident. Do you remember that?"

Harriett struggled to get back up into a fully upright position. She had been slumping down in her seat ever since passing out. The seatbelt was the only thing keeping her from ending up in a crumpled heap on the floorboard. Turning her attention toward the windshield, her eyes grew wide when she spotted Jose out in the rain, changing the tire. The headlights lit him up in a dull yellow glow, and his eyes glimmered when he looked up at us.

"No...I...oh wait. Did something...run in front of the car?" She seemed to be searching her memory for details of what had happened to us. "A raccoon?"

"No, not a raccoon. A squirrel...I think. It was nowhere big enough to be a raccoon. But you do remember, so that's good," I replied, pointing. "You swerved and we hit those rocks in front of us."

"Oh. Yeah, I do remember. Did that knock me out? How long have I been out?"

I shrugged. "I guess that's what happened. You've only been out a few minutes. Maybe a half hour." I picked up her soda. "Here, have a drink. You must be really tired from driving. Maybe the caffeine will perk you up." I bit my lip as she retrieved it from my hand and took a long drink.

"Why is he looking at us? It's creepy," Harriett asked. "I don't like him."

"I know. Me neither," I admitted.

"As soon as he's done," Harriett began, "we should just drive away."

I looked at her and smiled. It wasn't like the thought hadn't crossed my mind. But I needed to be the voice of reason, for the time being anyway. "We can't do that. It wouldn't be right. We can't be the people who let someone change our tire in the middle of the night, in the rain, and then just leaves him here. I may be a lot of things, but I wouldn't feel right about that."

Besides, I was making plans for getting rid of Jose in a much more fun way.

Harriett's face scrunched up and her eyes rolled up to the roof of the car. "Fine. We won't leave him here, if that's what you want." Her words said one thing, her voice told me she wasn't happy about it at all.

We felt the car bounce as Jose used the jack to lower it back down onto the new tire. After tightening the lug nuts, he stood and walked around, tossing the jack, lug wrench, and flat tire into the trunk of the car, before slamming it shut. I expected the passenger door to open a few seconds later, but it never did.

Turning, I watched as he jogged into the forest and disappeared behind a thick grove of trees. "What the…"

Harriett laughed. "He's probably just taking a leak."

"Oh yeah, I guess that's true," I replied.

"Last chance," Harriett told me. "If we are going to leave, we need to do it now. Are you sure you want to wait on him?"

"Yeah, I'm sure. He'll die out there. We can't leave him."

I could barely believe the words coming from my mouth. I didn't care about Jose. I had no attachment to him whatsoever. Yet…even though I wanted to be the one to kill him, and I knew I would get great pleasure out of it, I just couldn't leave him out there to suffer all night. It just wasn't who I was. So yes, I was positive that I didn't want to just drive away and leave him stranded.

CHAPTER 10

JOSE

I finished up with the tire changing. My hands were red and I was losing the feeling in my fingers by the time I was done. Rubbing them together to try to get the circulation going again, was slow work. None of it mattered though. My entire body was freezing, so a few numb fingers didn't change much.

After I threw everything back into the trunk, I went into the forest to relieve myself. I didn't turn around, but I could feel the eyes of Harriett and Autumn on me as I disappeared into the trees. It was probably a good thing that the forest was dense, otherwise the women would be getting more of a show than they bargained for. I silently prayed that they wouldn't drive away, leaving me stranded in the forest. I hurried with my task, not wanting to give them much of a chance to contemplate that very thing.

Once done, I ran and yanked the passenger door open, jumping into the backseat. "Holy crap, it's freezing out there.

My hands are frozen and I could barely open the door. Can you turn up the heat?"

Harriett reached over and once again twisted the dial as far as it would go. It still took several minutes before I felt any tiny bit of feeling in my fingers. Without asking if anyone minded, I pulled off my t-shirt and hung it over the seat in front of me. Autumn's eyes gravitated toward it and then toward me. She cocked her head to one side and shook it ever so slightly. Did I care? Nope. It was warmer without the dripping shirt on, than with it.

I looked around for something to dry off with, and found a t-shirt crumpled in the back floorboard. I grabbed it and wiped the rainwater from my skin. It helped a bit. Tossing the now wet t-shirt back onto the floor, it was finally time that I asked the question that had been burning a hole through me from the second Harriett pulled over and Autumn offered me a ride.

"Hey. Have either of you ever killed anyone?" I smiled in the dark backseat, knowing they couldn't see the expression on my face.

"Excuuuse me?" Harriett drawled out her words dramatically.

Autumn snapped her head around. I couldn't even describe the look on her face if I tried. It seemed like a mixture of disgust and delight. Hey, maybe I can describe it after all.

I looked back over at Harriett. "You heard me. Have you ever killed anyone?" I asked again.

"Of course not," Harriett replied. "What kind of question is that?"

"It's a serious one," I told her. "Lots of people have killed someone. Sometimes it's in self-defense. Sometimes it's in the heat of the moment, you know, like a lover's quarrel.

Sometimes it's plain old pre-meditated murder. There are many reasons to kill."

"Well, that's just disgusting," Harriett replied. "I don't know anyone who has ever killed anyone."

"Sure you do," I answered back.

"And how would you know? You don't know anyone that I know." She sounded so matter-of-fact that it almost made me sad to burst her sanctimonious bubble.

"You know me. Well…sort of anyway," I explained.

I watched as recognition dawned. Her face went from scrunched up confusion at my response, to complete understanding.

"Are you saying…?" I don't think she could get the words out. "Are you saying that you…? Oh, I don't even know what to say."

During all this time, Autumn sat conspicuously silent.

"It's okay, you can say it," I told her. "Yes, I've killed someone. Several someones actually." I folded my arms in front of me and grinned. "Does that shock you?"

They didn't know the half of it. When I said that I've killed several people, I wasn't exaggerating. I have left a bloody trail of drivers and vagrants all over the country. No, I haven't killed every single person who I've run into, but a good majority of them never made it to their destination. And I've been doing it since I was 14 and started on my travels.

I didn't intend to end anyone's life. It just happened. I only wanted to get to my next destination. But the third man to give me a ride…it was always a man, as women weren't so trusting, until now, that is. Harriett was the first woman to actually pull over for me. Anyway, that man annoyed the hell out of me. He spent probably an hour bragging about how he kept his wife and children in line. I guess he thought it was all anonymous telling a complete stranger intimate details of his abuse toward his family. I just sat there, letting him speak, hoping that he would move on to another topic. But no...it was all he wanted to talk about.

After a while, I just couldn't take it anymore. I used to be that little kid who was terrified of his father. It just wasn't in me to let what that man was doing to go unchallenged. When I told him that he was a complete asshole for what he was doing to his family, and that someone should do the same to him, his demeanor changed. Instead of smiling and appearing proud of his actions, his face took on a more sinister tone. Even the air in the car seemed to turn thick and ominous. Though he never said a word, the threat was real.

I was going to be next. He couldn't take the chance that I would tell someone...anyone...about what he had been doing. That was when he pulled over the car.

My body began to shake. But I didn't hesitate. If I had, I would most likely be dead right now. I jumped out of the car and ran. The dark night provided the much needed cover I prayed for. He had pulled over next to a large cornfield and I blindly ran in, hoping to just hide long enough for him to give up and leave.

That didn't happen.

He took chase. I ducked down one of the rows and tried not to move. I barely took a breath, thinking he might hear me.

A gun shot rang out. "Hey boy! Get your ass out here where I can see you or I'm going to kill you. You have nowhere to go!"

It was a big cornfield and I knew that it might take a long time before he found me. If ever. I held my ground.

Another gun shot. That's when I began worrying that his random shooting might just hit me. I needed to come up with a plan. And fast.

I waited until he walked past me. He was still yelling and

threatening my life. Before he realized what was happening, I pounced onto his back. We both went down in a tangled heap. The gun flew out of his hand and was lost in the never ending dirt of the cornfield. It was very dark out and neither of us would probably ever find that gun. Not that it mattered. We were suddenly in a life and death struggle. The gun all but forgotten.

I was on the man's back, while he struggled to turn over. I wrapped a forearm around the front of his throat and pulled. It made it tough for him to breathe, but not impossible. It wouldn't hold him back for long. That was something I was sure of.

I didn't have any plans beyond the initial pounce. Now what? I thought. I had no weapon and the man outweighed me by a good sixty pounds or more. It wouldn't be long until he was able to throw me off and probably kill me on the spot.

I needed to think quickly. In a moment, the perfect solution came to me. I grabbed the dirty yellow bandana that was loosely tied around my neck. A bit awkwardly, I managed to get it around his neck. I squeezed with everything I had. He lost all reasoning and clawed at the item that was cutting off his ability to breathe. Had he just reached back and gouged me in the eyes, the struggle would have been over. But I don't think people have that reasoning when their lives are in immediate danger.

He gasped for breath. My mind went to his family. His wife, who would no longer bear the bruises of his fury. The children, who would no longer cower when he walked into the room. The peace and serenity that would forever fill their house after that night. Yeah, I was doing the right thing.

Of course, I can't say it was all an altruistic act on my part. I was also trying to survive. The man had been shooting wildly into a cornfield a night, after all. Even if he couldn't see where I was, a stray bullet could find its way to me. I couldn't take that chance.

I could feel the man losing his battle with consciousness. He was no longer gasping for breath and his hands dropped to his side. When his head slumped forward, I knew it was all over.

Releasing the bandana from around his neck, his face planted into the dirt below us. I climbed off of his back and retied the bandana around my neck. Fishing his car keys from his pocket, I wandered back to his car and drove off into the night. I hadn't even bothered to try to hide his body. No one on the road would be able to see him. But he might be a surprise to the corn farmer the next day.

I abandoned the car a day later. No sense in taking the chance of being found in the car of a dead guy.

That was the first person I ever killed. But he certainly was not the last. Being out on the road, I had to defend myself a lot. And I had killed many people. It wasn't always in self-defense. I can't claim that. Once I killed a hobo for a couple of cans of food he was hoarding. Don't judge me. I promise that you would do almost anything to survive when you are starving.

Now, it's kind of second nature to me to kill those who need to be killed. For whatever reason it may be...

Harriett's voice snapped me back to reality. "Well...yes. That's really shocking," she responded. I was so engrossed in reliving the cornfield story that I had almost forgotten I had asked her if me killing people shocked her.

She turned to Autumn. "Don't you have anything to say about this?" Then she leaned in so that she could whisper into Autumn's ear. "It was your idea to pick him up."

"You know that I can hear you, right?" I laughed from the back seat.

Still, Autumn said nothing.

"Well, I guess we should head out now." Harriett reached down to start the car.

"Are you sure you are in shape to drive?" I asked. "I mean, you were passed out not long ago, and you look a bit drowsy even now." I turned to Autumn. She gave no indication of even hearing my words. "Autumn, do you have anything to say?"

She shrugged, without turning to face me. "Like what?"

"Like, don't you think it's a bad idea for her to drive?"

"I don't know, maybe."

"Maybe? That's all you have to say?" I was appalled. I was also pretty damn sure that Autumn slipped something into Harriett's drink, which explained why Harriett was so out of it. "I know what you did." There...I said it.

She turned around and looked at me finally. "What are you talking about?"

"Don't play games with me," I replied. "You know exactly what I'm talking about. I saw you put something in Harriett's drink."

Harriett's head swiveled to look directly at Autumn. "You did what?! Is that why I'm so sleepy and out of it? You drugged me? And you just handed it to me and said that the caffeine would wake me up."

Autumn sucked in her breath and turned back to Harriett. "What? No, I didn't drug you," Autumn replied. "That jackass is making things up and trying to cause trouble. I had a headache and I put some aspirin in my own soda. I put nothing in yours."

"Liar," I spat from the back seat. "I stood there in the store and watched you."

"Yeah, I just told you that I put something in my own drink. I'm not the one who is a killer here." She narrowed her eyes my way.

I ignored that last comment. It was true, I had just

admitted that fact. But we could get into that later. "Like I said, you are a liar." I wasn't about to back down. I knew for a fact what had actually happened. And it wasn't a bit of aspirin in her own drink.

"I can't believe you did that," Harriett told Autumn. "Why would you want to drug me?"

"I didn't! Don't tell me you actually believe that guy over me. Especially after what he just admitted to us. Besides, maybe he put something in your drink. He took the cups from me in the store." Autumn looked back at me with a barely perceptible smile. Harriett didn't notice.

Harriett stared at Autumn. I could see that she was contemplating her next move. "Ugh, I don't even know what to believe now."

"Believe me," Autumn told her. "He," she pointed toward me with only her thumb over her shoulder, "is just trying to cause trouble between us. For all I know, he's the one who drugged you. It certainly wasn't me. I know that much for sure."

Harriett reached for the ignition switch once more. "Let's just go. I want to get this trip over as soon as humanly possible."

"You know," Autumn said directly to me, "perhaps this is a good spot for you to get out and continue on your own way."

She stared at me, unblinking. My eyes widened.

"Are you serious? You want to kick me out in the middle of the night? It's raining and freezing out there, and I just risked my own life to change the tire on a car that isn't even mine." I couldn't believe what I was hearing. Okay…maybe I could believe it. I mean, I did just tell the two of them that I was a killer.

"Yes, I do, actually. You are sitting back there accusing me of drugging someone, when you have no proof. I don't know what your end game is, but I want no part of it."

Autumn didn't look like she was even close to backing down.

"Perhaps you should both get out," Harriett offered. "I was just trying to help you both with a ride tonight, but look what it's gotten me. It got me drugged," she looked directly at Autumn, "and it got me into an accident. And for all I know, it's going to get me killed." That one was aimed directly at me.

"How is some animal scurrying across the road anyone's fault?" Autumn challenged. "And for the hundredth time, I didn't drug you."

Harriett pointed toward the side of the road. "Get out. Both of you."

CHAPTER 11

HARRIETT

The heater was still on full blast, yet I shivered in the hot car. Jose finally finished changing the tire, and then announced that Autumn drugged me. I don't know why I would believe a complete stranger, but I did believe him. I wasn't just tired from hours of driving. It was more than that. Way more. I felt the overwhelming grogginess that I get whenever I take a sleeping pill. Yeah, I believed that someone had slipped me something. Of course, I couldn't be entirely sure of who that someone was. Autumn seemed like the obvious suspect, since she was the one who brought me the soda. As far as I knew, Jose hadn't had any direct contact with it. So, yeah, Autumn had to be the one.

Then he had the audacity to ask if either of us had ever killed anyone, and admitted that he had. Of course I denied it. It would be stupid to do otherwise. He didn't have to know that my body count was well into the double digits.

But I'm not a bad person. Really I'm not. I know, I know,

admitting to killing dozens of people would seem to prove otherwise, but I don't always kill just for the fun of it. Sometimes I kill to get rid of the scourges of humanity.

Someone's got to do it.

It was all I could do to not howl with laughter when the topic of the Black River killer came up. And just for the record, no, I'm not the River Killer. Well…not the only one, if I'm being completely honest.

I've killed several people in Black River. But so has someone else. And I know who that someone else is. I'm pretty sure that I'm the only one who knows this. It has been a mystery in that town for more than thirty years. The sheriff, who lost his cousin to the River Killer, hasn't had any luck figuring out who he is.

I witnessed the River Killer stabbing someone in the woods late one night. I couldn't sleep and was out for a stroll on the river path, just trying to clear my head, when I heard a commotion nearby. There was a person lying on the ground, with the killer straddling her mid-section. And stabbing. Oh my god, the stabbing. It was a horrific thing to watch. When I kill someone, I'm in the zone and not really thinking about the ramifications of what I'm doing. It is so much more horrifying when watching someone else do it.

I recognized the killer immediately, even from a bit of a distance. I have never told anyone. I didn't want to have to explain what I was doing out there late at night, and possibly even be accused of the crime myself. So I kept quiet. But, I've spent a lot of my free time watching the killer. It's funny how someone can just go about their life on a daily basis and seem completely innocent of anything.

When I return to Black River, I may have to have it out with the killer. I don't want them to mess up my own plans. Yeah, they have to go.

I glanced over at Autumn, who was trying to get that

short blonde hair of hers to stand up, instead of lying flat on her head. It was a comical mess. The rain and weather will do that.

I do have to admit, that the moment I saw pathetic looking Autumn sitting in front of the convenience store, in the state I found her in, I got all tingly inside. I wanted nothing more than to wrap my hands around her neck and put her out of her misery. Then once she told me that she was from Black River, I was thrilled.

Unfortunately, once she yelled for me to pull over and pick Jose up, I knew that killing her was probably not going to happen. At least not until he went on his way, that is, or we got back to Black River. I should have kept on driving. Stopping was my first mistake.

What was my second mistake, you ask? That would be telling Autumn and Jose to get out of my car. That didn't go over very well at all.

Autumn. That teenager who was a mess when I first came across her, the one who had bruises and cuts on her face, along with blood on her shirt, she was the one who responded in the most intense way.

I honestly thought that Jose would be the one to react. He was the one who told us he had killed people. So why did I think I was any different? Any better? I didn't. He was the one I leaned away from, hoping it would be difficult for him to get a hold of me.

But he didn't move. He sat quietly in the backseat and made no indication that he had even heard me.

It was Autumn who surprised me when she jumped on me. It happened so quickly and so unexpectedly, that I wasn't ready for her. I was ready for Jose, not Autumn.

The girl began punching and scratching at me. In my less than stellar state, since I had almost definitely been drugged, I struggled to defend myself. I was already in a tight space, sitting in the driver's seat, with the steering wheel taking up much of the room. With the crazy girl on top of me, I found myself scooting lower and lower in my seat. After a minute or so, I was lying completely on my back, and I couldn't get any further away from her.

I did my best to fight back, but Autumn had the upper hand. Her surprise attack left me almost defenseless. I cried out in pain when her claw of a hand swiped across my face. I didn't have to reach up to know that blood was dripping from the open wound.

Suddenly, Autumn lifted completely off of me in one fell swoop. The wide eyes and gaped mouth told me that it wasn't of her own doing.

"Okay, that's enough!" I heard Jose yell.

He had flung Autumn into the backseat and she was sitting next to him when I finally managed to get myself back up into a seated position. I glared at the girl as I reached across the seat to the glovebox, in search of a napkin. Fishing one out, I pressed it to my left cheek to stop the blood.

"What the hell?" I finally asked Autumn, as calmly as I could muster.

"You have no right to kick us out!" Autumn yelled back.

I took a deep breath before responding. "Excuse me, but I'm pretty sure this is my car, and I have every right to kick you out whenever I feel like it."

Autumn looked out the window next to her. "It's the middle of the damn night, and it's raining out there. We would freeze to death. You can't do that, you would be killing us." She folded her arms in front of her chest. It was a defiant move. "I can't speak for him," she glanced over at Jose, "but I'm not going anywhere, and you can't make me."

Wanna bet, I thought to myself.

CHAPTER 12

AUTUMN

Someone grabbed me around the waist and yanked me off of Harriett. It didn't immediately register in my brain who had a hold on me, or exactly what was going on before I was flung over the backseat and set roughly down next to Jose.

I couldn't believe what I was hearing. Jose and I were both being kicked out into the night. But before I had a chance to even contemplate the implications of that, I decided right then and there that I had had enough. Harriett was not going to get away with it. I didn't care that it was her car. I didn't care if she liked either one of us or not. No, I didn't care one bit about any of it. That woman was not going to make us leave the warmth and safety of her car. I had absolutely no intention of dying of hypothermia, or anything else for that matter. Just hell no.

After she told us that it was her car and that she had every right to kick us out if she felt like it, I could almost feel the steam coming out of my ears. Of course, the fight we just had didn't help matters. But it certainly made me feel better. I had gotten in a few good licks. Harriett barely fought back. I had her pinned down in her seat, with the door, seat, and steering wheel blocking her in. She had nowhere to go, and very little room to defend herself.

I liked it that way.

I turned to face Jose. "Why did you do that? I had her exactly where I wanted her."

"You might have killed her if I hadn't intervened."

Smiling, "Yeah, that was kind of the point."

"And then what? Open the door and kick her body out onto the side of the road, and just be on our merry way?" he asked. The snark in his voice was not lost on me.

I shrugged. "Yeah, something like that."

"Don't be stupid."

I tilted my head to the side, trying to size him up. What was his game? Was there a plan in that head of his? Maybe he was the one who wanted to do the killing. It wasn't like he hadn't already admitted that he had killed a lot of people. Funny. If he only knew what I was capable of.

Harriett began yelling at me from the front seat. I watched as she pulled a tissue out of the glove compartment and held it against her cheek. That made me smile. I hadn't managed to kill her, but I wounded her pretty good. She could kick us out if she felt like it?

No she couldn't. Really.

I had no intention of going anywhere, and I told her so. After what had just happened, I wondered if she actually thought she could do anything about it. Especially since there were two of us. She couldn't force both of us out.

Suddenly, her eyelids got really heavy. She struggled to keep them open. I howled with laughter, causing both Harriett and Jose to look at me in bewilderment.

"Why don't you have some more soda? It oughta help wake you up," I told her.

Harriett looked down at the cup sitting in the holder between the two front seats, and back up at me. "You did put something in it, didn't you?"

I shrugged. "Maybe. Maybe not."

Jose gave me a knowing look, but said nothing.

"Fantastic," she replied. "I'm such an idiot. I know better than to pick up two hitchhikers. Yep, this is all on me."

"I'm not arguing with you on that one," I told her with a grin. Turning to Jose, "And why are you so quiet? You got nothing to say?"

"Nope. I'm just here to stay out of the rain."

"You're an idiot," I told him point blank. "We should have left you out there to freeze to death."

With that, I crawled back over the seat and made myself comfortable in the front passenger seat. "Come on, let's go," I told Harriett.

Before I realized what was happening, I felt something wrap around my neck and squeeze, knocking the breath out of me. My hands instinctively reached to grasp whatever it was that had a hold of me. It was wrapped so tightly, that I couldn't get my fingers underneath it. Oh god, gasping for air that wouldn't come was the worst thing that I could possibly imagine at that moment. I watched stars swimming in my vision.

CHAPTER 13

JOSE

After I pulled Autumn off of Harriett, the stupid girl began to argue with Harriett, and then with me. When she called me an idiot, and crawled over into the front seat, I had had enough. The girl was annoying and causing more trouble for me than she knew. Drugging Harriett's drink was tremendously stupid on her part. She could have gotten both of us killed. I couldn't have that. I was done with her.

I needed to act fast, before Harriett started the car and drove away. Carefully, and without tearing my eyes from either person in the front seat, I untied the yellow bandana from around my neck. It had seen better days, I know that, but it was a gift from a young woman who I loved once. Though she is now somewhere three or four feet under the desert floor, I really did love her. I paused to think about that. If she just hadn't betrayed me…

There was no time for lamenting over lost loves now. I had a task to complete.

The bandana came loose just as Autumn instructed Harriett to get moving again. It was now or never. Before Autumn had a chance to realize what was going on, I wrapped the bandana around her neck, in one swift move, and pulled. I pulled so hard that I had to press my knees up against the seat in front of me for leverage.

It took the girl several seconds to realize what was happening. I didn't need to see her face to know exactly what was going through her mind. At first, something was on her neck. Then she felt it tighten. Then she couldn't breathe. That's when it hit her that I was strangling her, and there wasn't anything she could do about it. Not a damn thing.

Oh, she tried to pull the bandana off. But it wasn't going anywhere. And I was positive that it was only moments before her world started going dark. That made me smile.

Until Harriett got involved, that is. With a scream, she got up on her knees on the seat and pounced. The woman started hitting me. But that wasn't even the worst part. The hitting I could handle. It was the screeching that went along with it. She was only inches from me and I thought the screeching might pierce my eardrum.

I held on tightly to the bandana and turned to face Harriett. With the most savage face I could muster, I spoke directly to her, with gritted teeth. "You had better back off, and I mean right now."

It didn't seem to phase Harriett. "Let her go!" she screamed, still punching me and pulling at the bandana. "You are going to kill her!"

All the while, Autumn was gurgling and the fight was leaving her body.

"Why do you want me to stop?" I asked Harriett. "She drugged you with god knows what, and you want me to let her live? For all we know that was poison in your cup."

Harriett instinctively looked down to where the cup in

question was now on its side between her and Autumn. It had been knocked over in the struggle.

And then something changed. Something came over Harriett. I saw it the moment it happened. Resignation is the best word that I can come up with.

The fury on her face was replaced with sadness. She stopped hitting me, and even released the bandana that she had been digging at. She then sat back in the driver's seat of her car and stared ahead. Harriett said nothing. Even I, being the person that I am, was surprised at her abrupt about face.

While watching Harriett, I hadn't realized that I was loosening my grip on the dirty yellow bandana. Suddenly, Autumn gasped for air and struggled once again. I had no choice but to pull as tightly as I could manage on the noose around her neck. A few seconds later, it was all over. Even so, I still held on for another minute. I needed to be sure.

Once the deed had been done, I unwrapped it and placed the dirty yellow bandana once again around my neck and tied it. It hung loosely as if taunting anyone who dared cross me.

Autumn's body slumped in the front seat. Harriett turned briefly and looked at her. There was no expression on her face. I couldn't tell if this was something she had witnessed before, or if she was in total shock from the whole thing. Did she worry that I would come after her next?

"What now?" Harriett asked me, without turning to look my way.

"Help me get her out of the car and into the forest," I ordered. And I said it in a way that made it crystal clear that it was not up for debate. She would get out and help me. The woman did know first hand what I was capable of.

I didn't really need the help. I could have easily hefted the waif of a teenager over my shoulder and done away with her on my own. But I needed Harriett to get out of the car. There was no doubt whatsoever in my mind that she would take off the moment I got Autumn out. So no, I wasn't about to be stupid enough to let that happen.

CHAPTER 14

HARRIETT

Oh god, he just killed Autumn. I'm probably next. Yeah, I've killed, but I've never had anyone try to kill me before. The feeling was surreal. He hadn't tried anything with me yet, but I knew it was coming. I just knew. There was no reason for him to keep me alive, especially with what I had just witnessed.

I couldn't take my eyes off of poor Autumn's body, lying in a heap, partially in the passenger seat and partially in the floorboard. My body began shaking, and it wasn't from the cold. It was fear. Horrible, crippling fear. I briefly wondered if this was what my victims felt at the moment they realized they were not going to be alive much longer. Interesting. And, oh god, so terrifying.

I jolted out of my trance at the harshness of Jose's voice. "Help me get her out of the car and into the forest."

Did he say that just to lure me out into the woods, so he

could murder me too? Maybe I should open my car door and run as fast as I could into the night. I thought about that, and what a bad idea that was. First, it was raining and the middle of the night. If he didn't catch me, I would freeze to death in an hour. That was something I was sure of. Second, Jose was much younger and faster than I was. I had never actually seen him run, but I was no athlete. I was a 40 year old heft of a woman. A teenage boy would have no trouble outrunning me. Yep, I would be down in seconds.

So, now what? Help him? If I did, perhaps there was a chance, albeit a slim one, that he would let me live. It was probably my only hope.

"Did you hear me?!"

I jumped again at his voice. He was more insistent this time. I made my decision. "Yeah, okay, I'm coming."

I grabbed my coat and climbed out of the car, the biting wind and rain hit me hard. I shrugged into my coat quickly, but it didn't do a lot to help. I was already soaked. Then something dawned on me. The t-shirt that Autumn had been wearing was still lying in the back floorboard. It wouldn't keep me alive, but it would be forensic evidence if they ever found our bodies out in the forest. Jose had been in the backseat for a while, and had very likely gotten some of his DNA on it at some point. It seemed to be my only hope of him getting captured.

I quickly opened the back door, reached in, and grabbed the t-shirt. I threw it on the road beneath the car.

"What are you doing?" Jose snapped at me.

"I...was just...looking for my gloves." I slammed the car door. "They aren't here."

Running around to the other side of the car, I pulled open the passenger door. Poor Autumn must have been leaning against it, as she fell out of the car. Her lower half was in the passenger floorboard and her upper half was hanging out, with her head twisted at an almost impossible angle on the muddy side of the road.

I couldn't stifle my gasp. Jose was already out of the car and shook his head in disgust at me. I watched as the rain ran down his face and dripped off of his chin. He swiped at it with the back of his hand.

"I'll take her shoulders and you get her feet," he ordered.

I nodded, without speaking. It seemed imperative that I do whatever I could to stay alive. If that meant taking orders from a kid half my age, so be it. Minutes later, my heart beating a thousand beats per second, we entered the dense forest, dragging Autumn's body in.

It seemed as if I could barely breathe. Autumn wasn't that heavy, but trudging her through the muddy ground, around rocks and trees was exhausting. And I wasn't in the best shape to begin with. "Can we stop for a minute? I need to catch my breath," I asked. Jose was the one in charge, so asking his permission seemed like the logical thing to do.

"Good god, you aren't that old," he snarled. "Maybe if you were in better shape..." He didn't finish that sentence.

"It's not like I was expecting to be carrying dead weight through the mud, in the middle of the night," I shot back at him. "What exercise is needed for that?"

The look on his face caused me to shut my mouth immediately. I said nothing, but tried to convey the word 'sorry' with just my eyes. I don't think it was working.

"Put her down. We can stop for a minute."

I complied immediately, dropping Autumn's feet with a thud.

Not thirty seconds later, Jose spoke up. "Okay, long enough. Let's go."

"Go where?" I asked, looking up at Jose with questioning eyes.

"We need to go deeper in. I don't want her to be found anytime soon."

I took a deep breath, and complied, picking up her feet and heading further in. It was terrifying, thinking about the possibility that I would never leave that forest alive. My entire body was shaking uncontrollably by then. A moment later I lost my grip on her feet, and one of her shoes came off in my hand, as her feet hit the ground once again.

"What are you doing?" Jose bared his teeth at me. "Is that her shoe you're holding?" Without waiting for a response, he continued. "Throw that off into the trees and pick her feet back up. It's freezing out here, and I want to get back to the car."

I complied, heaving the shoe as far as I could into the trees. We both stood and watched it fly. Once done, I picked up Autumn's feet and we resumed our trek.

A few minutes later, Jose stopped. "This is fine. Let's put her behind these rocks. There's a lot of bushes here and she probably won't be found. Even if she is, they can't tie it back to us."

"Us?" The word came out of my mouth before I had a chance to think about it.

"Yeah, us," he replied. "You are involved in this too."

"But you are the one who killed her, not me." Why was I arguing with a cold blooded killer? My mouth was going to get me into trouble. I just knew it. I felt as if I was already going to die by his hands. There was no need to make it worse, especially if I had even the slightest chance of making it out of this alive.

Jose dropped Autumn's body behind the rocks. "Can you prove that I was the one who killed her?" He didn't wait for an answer. "No, you can't. That makes you culpable."

I ignored his idea of logic. Though Autumn had attacked me not so long ago, and scratched me up pretty good, I felt badly for the girl. I knelt down and smoothed her hair that was in a tangle around her head and face. I also placed her hands on top of each other on her belly.

She looked so peaceful. That's when I realized that I didn't even know her last name. I couldn't let her family know where she was, even anonymously. Not that it would have been a good idea to do so anyway. The last thing I needed was to get in the middle of a murder investigation.

"Come on, let's go," Jose ordered.

"Where are we going now?" I asked, standing up to face him. We were about the same height, but he seemed so much more imposing to me, now that we were standing face to face. I couldn't help but shrink down just a bit. The man scared me.

"We," he made an all inclusive gesture with his hand, "are not going anywhere. This is where it all ends for you."

My eyes widened. "Wha…what… do you…mean?" I could barely get the words out. It was a stupid question.

"You know what I mean," he told me. And I did.

Without thinking, I took off in a dead run. I had no idea where I was going, but I had to try. If I didn't, then I would just be giving up. I couldn't do that. I had to give it my best effort.

I was turned around and was pretty sure that I was running deeper into the forest. But it was better than the alternative.

I was never going to outrun a young man, half my age. I was under no illusion that it was even possible. But…just maybe…I could find somewhere to hide in the dark forest. There were tons of boulders and trees, and even ravines. Surely I could find one of them to conceal me. And with the dark gloomy night, I was sure that I could hide from him. He would never find me, or so I hoped.

My breathing became labored and I slowed down. I couldn't run if I couldn't breathe. I darted behind a tree and pressed my back up against it, doing my best to not wheeze with every intake of air.

CHAPTER 15

JOSE

"Dammit!"

I made the mistake of telling Harriett that I was about to kill her. She took off running into the forest. What did I expect? Now I was going to have to chase her. And I was already freezing.

The woman was fast, I had to give her that. I guess running for your life will make even the slowest person into a gold medal sprinter. She disappeared into the trees before I had the chance to go after her. But now the chase was on. I took off in the direction that I had last seen her go in.

It didn't take long until I found her…or heard her to be exact. I couldn't see her, but she was close by, I was sure of it. She might have been fast, but I was younger and faster. She didn't have a chance. There was a full moon that night, but the clouds decided to cover it up for the most part, only leaving a dull glow all around us. Even though it was quite dark out, and I had a hard time seeing her, being able to hear her was quite helpful. The forest floor was really soggy, but the branches and leaves still crunched under her feet. Unless she tiptoed her way through, she couldn't get through the forest quietly. It just wasn't possible.

On the other hand, she could hear me too, and knew exactly where I was, of that I was sure. This made for an interesting chase. It made the whole thing a little bit more fun. Though I could have done without the rain.

Without breaking stride, Harriett looked over her left shoulder and sped up her pace. I could hear her wheezing from twenty feet behind her. That quicker speed didn't last long and she began to falter. I couldn't see her well, but I was able to catch of glimpse of her as she ducked behind a tree.

I smiled.

Within seconds, I pounced.

The two of us landed on the ground in a heap. Her on her belly. Me on her back. She began to scream. It didn't matter. There was not a soul in the forest who would hear her. She could scream to her heart's content. I climbed to a seated position, straddling her back. She flung her arms, and tried to push herself up and me with her. But I wasn't going anywhere. Yes, she outweighed me, but I was stronger. I had no problem keeping her down.

Strangling her seemed so anti-climatic. I had just done that with Autumn and it was kind of…boring. I needed to quickly come up with an alternate plan. I fished around in my pockets for my knife. "Dammit," I uttered. It wasn't there. I was sure that it was now among the myriad of items lost forever in the dark forest.

So, now what? Snapping her neck was a possibility. But let me tell you, I've tried it, and it's not as easy as it is in the movies. A quick twist of the head and someone's neck is broken, causing them to fall to the ground, dead. Nope, not that easy.

Maybe something nearby I could use as a weapon? I perused the area for just the perfect thing. It was only drizzling by then, but it was still pretty dark. My eyes had adjusted somewhat, but seeing very far from our spot on the ground, was difficult.

Harriett had slowed down her struggle, probably due to the exhaustion of running for her life. That was fine with me. I was tired also, and not in the mood for more struggling.

I spied a softball sized rock and leaned over to pick it up. She must have seen me do that, because she began screaming and fighting with all of her might to buck me off of her.

She was stronger than I expected, and caused me to lose my hold on her. I flew sideways, tumbling off of her back. Before I had a chance to realize exactly what had happened, she scrambled to her feet and took off like a shot, once again. The funny thing was that she continued screaming as she ran.

"Ah, for the love of god!" I jumped up and went after her. Unfortunately for her, I was even more pissed off and had caught my second wind. I reached her within seconds. Again, we went down. This time I didn't fool around. I couldn't risk her escaping again. While running I had held fast onto the rock.

The moment it made contact with her skull, the screaming ceased. It was peaceful once again. She gurgled, and I smashed it into the back of her head for a second time. That cause her to go completely silent. Dead silent. The peacefulness of the night was heaven.

Climbing off of her back and kneeling beside her, I fished in her pockets for the car keys. Finding none, I surmised that she had left them in the ignition. At least I hoped she had. I would never be able to find them in the forest. There was so much debris on the ground that missing keys would stay that way for years.

I grabbed her legs and began dragging her. "Holy crap," I exclaimed. The woman was heavy. It took everything I had to get her to some nearby bushes. I silently cursed the fact that I had killed Autumn first. I could have used her help with Harriett's body right about then. Once I finally got her out of sight, I bent her legs up so that she was completely hidden. Only the animals would find her now.

Jogging back to the car, I did indeed find the keys still in the ignition. It was my lucky day.

I climbed into my new car and drove off into the night. I was heading to the town of Black River with mayhem on my mind. A smile graced my lips.

~

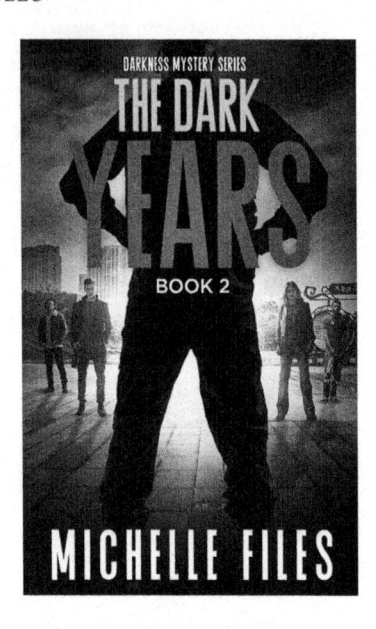

Get the exciting next book in the series to read all about the Black River Killer.

Jake Cavanaugh suspects that he knows the identity of the person who has been terrorizing the town of Black River for more than three decades. As he gets closer and closer to the truth, his life is in danger. Now he must confirm who the killer is so that he can save himself…and those around him.

Don't miss this unputdownable thriller.

Darkness Mystery Series:
- Escape the Dark - Book 1
- The Dark Years - Book 2
- The Children - Book 3
- Suspicions on River Road - Book 4
- Sapphire Valley - Book 5
- Family on Fire - Book 6

Author Note

Thank you for reading my book. As an author, your support is extremely important. If you liked this book, please leave a great review on the site you purchased it from. And please consider reading one of my other titles. :-)

If you enjoyed this book and would like information on new releases, sign up for my newsletter here:

www.MichelleFiles.com

Printed in Dunstable, United Kingdom